For Mommy.
With thanks to Shadra.

GUS
and the GREATEST
CATCH OF ALL

Victoria Cossack

PAGE
STREET
KIDS

#1 FISHER

Gus was the very best fisherman in town, no contest—

although he'd won many.

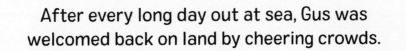

After every long day out at sea, Gus was
welcomed back on land by cheering crowds.

He had everything a fisherman could ask for:
talent, success, and a full fishing net.
Thanks to his clever fishing tactics, he caught
twenty-five fish each day. But he wanted more.

He wanted to be world-famous.
And he had a perfect plan.

He would catch a record-breaking one hundred fish,
quadrupling his usual number!

He suited up, gathered his equipment,
and called up every single news station he could.

With the cameras rolling, Gus dumped an entire
bucket of bait into the water. He assured everyone that
it wouldn't be long until his net was overflowing.

Fish appeared one by one, but they were coming in quicker than Gus had anticipated.

The school of fish was growing by the second.

Gus hadn't even had a chance to catch a single one when his boat began to rock beneath him.

It shook back and forth, harder and harder, until . . .

SPLASH!

His hat, rod, and net were lost in the blue.
Taking a great big breath just in time,
Gus plummeted into the water.

Once his eyes adjusted, all Gus could see were fish.
Fish everywhere. *This is my chance*, he thought.
One hundred fish!

He frantically tried to snatch as many fish as he could,
but they were just too quick and slippery.

The fish thought it was a bit rude of Gus to grab at them.
They expected more smarts from such a clever fisherman.
They gestured for Gus to follow them.

Gus, never one to turn down a competition, did.
He was determined to find another chance
to catch them when they least expected it.

The school of fish guided Gus through a colorful
coral reef that he had no time to appreciate.
Before he could plot another attack,

some seagrass tickled his behind,
and he lost his focus.

Then he thought he might get close enough to
catch the fish if he challenged them to some games.

They played tag,

charades,

and even chess.

Despite Gus's best efforts, the fish won every time.
And the more he played, the less he thought about his goal.

Gus realized that if he scooped up all the fish,
he would no longer have anybody to play with.

He started to think that having one hundred new friends
might be better than catching a record-breaking one hundred fish.
These fish were rather fun! So he kept following them until . . .

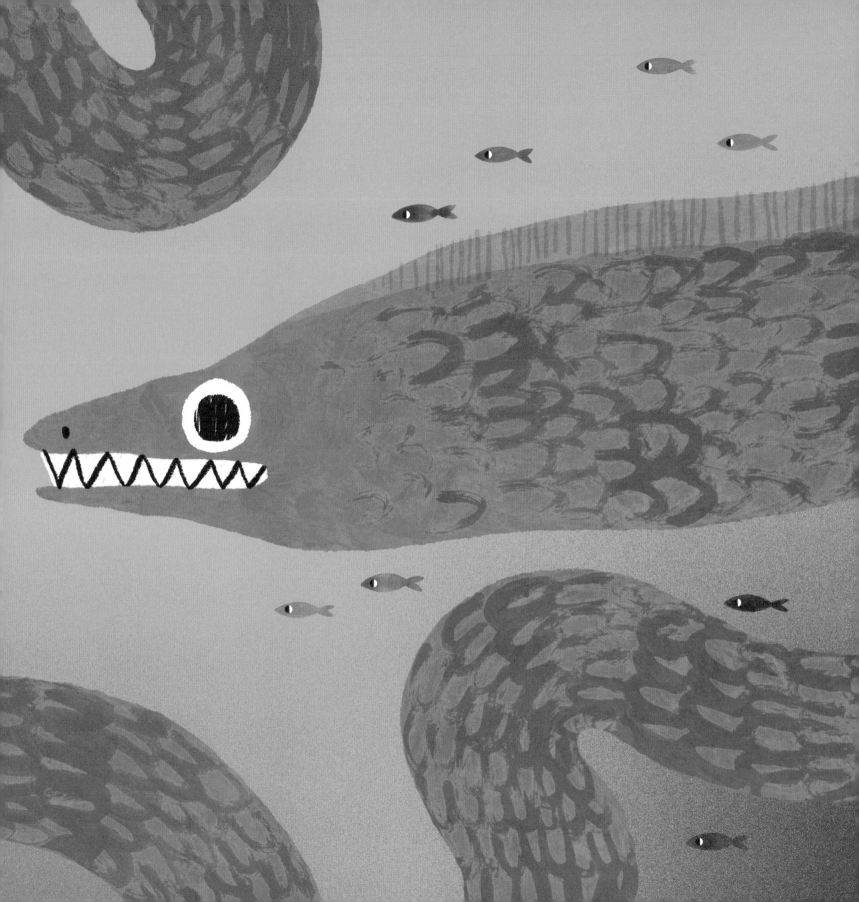

The fish had outsmarted him!
Gus's heart pounded, his eyes bulged, and he feared the worst.
Just when he was sure his life was over . . .

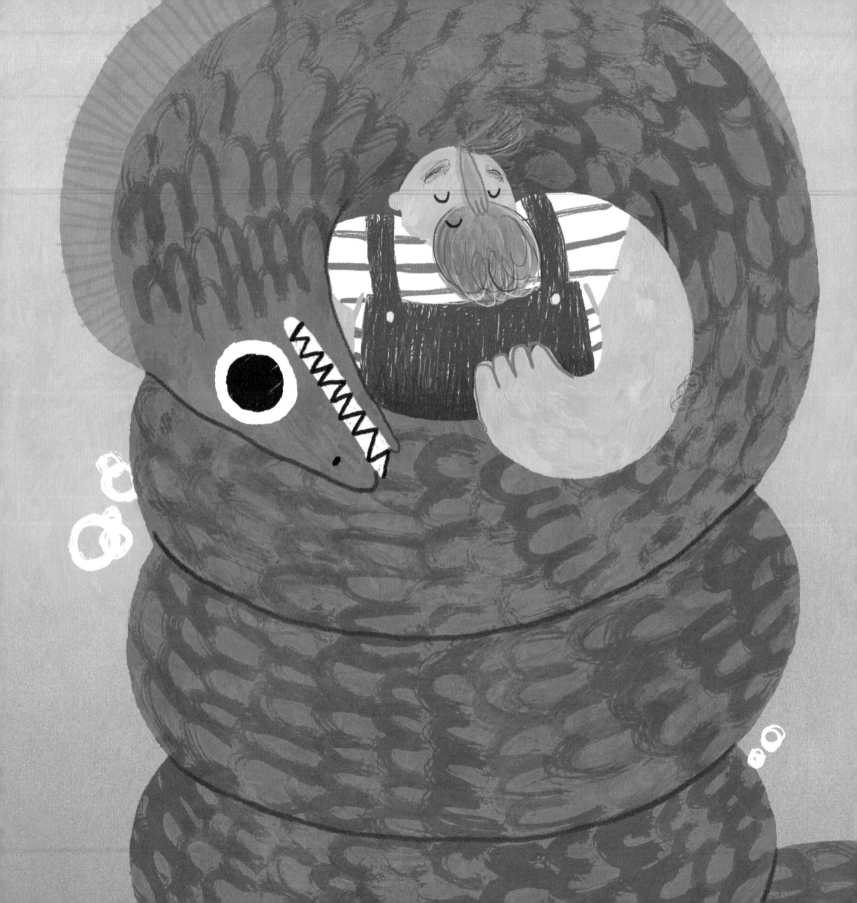

the squeeze began to feel warm.
And comforting.

Like a hug from a friend!

With all the excitement, Gus had lost track of time.
He told his new friends—a record-breaking 101!—
that he really should get going.

After all, he wasn't sure how much
longer he could hold his breath.

The fish were sad to see him go.

Gus headed toward home with a full heart and,
for the very first time, an empty fishing net.

By the time he was back on land,
the news teams and cameras were long gone.

He never did become a world-famous fisherman,

but he became the world's very
BEST FISH FRIEND.
And he thought that was the greatest catch of all.